Queen Gail Waits
and
Wait!

Written by
Georgie Tennant

Illustrated by
Simona Hodonova

Can you say this sound and draw it with your finger?

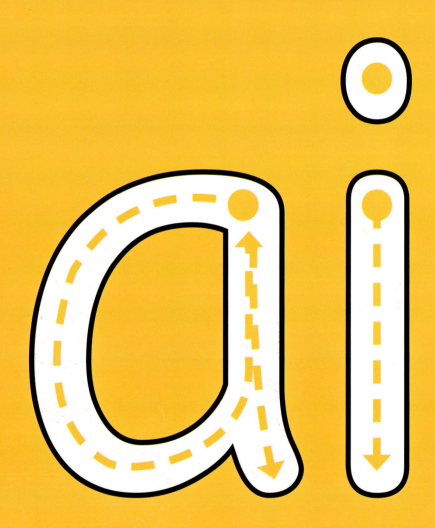

Queen Gail Waits

Written by
Georgie Tennant

Illustrated by
Simona Hodonova

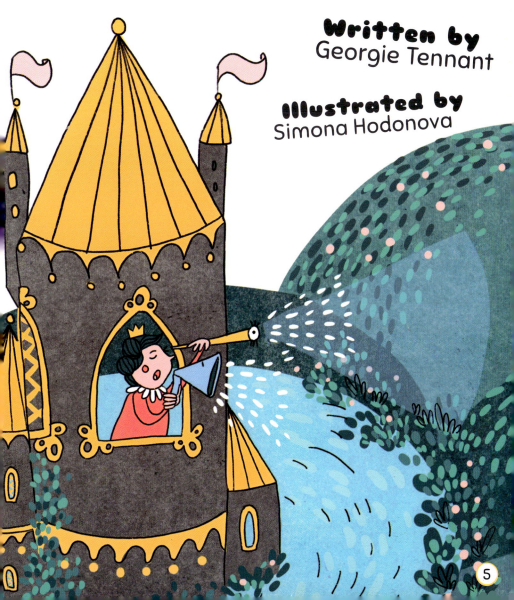

Queen Gail is in a keep. She waits.

The Sun is up. She waits and weeps.

The Sun sets. She wails then has a nap.

She can see a man!

It is King Zack. "Can you see me?" yells Queen Gail.

"I see you!" Zack yells back.
Queen Gail waits.

"I can not get to you!" he wails.
"Yes you can, Zack!"

It is deep. Zack can not feel his feet.

Queen Gail waits. It rains. "I will fail," Zack wails.

"Can you get this sheet?"
Zack waits. Queen Gail tugs.

King Zack is up. "I did not fail!"
he yells.

"I got you up! We are pals!"

Can you say this sound and draw it with your finger?

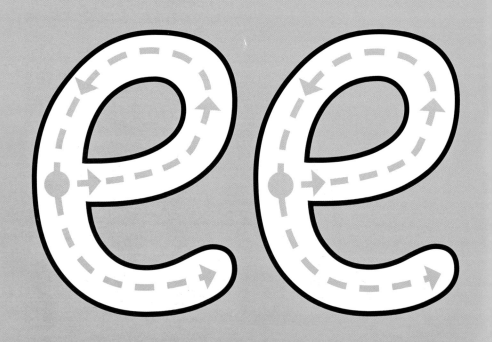

Wait!

Written by
Georgie Tennant

Illustrated by
Simona Hodonova

Ben and Sam are with Mum.
She needs to rush.

"Wait!" yells Sam. "I need my sheep!"

Mum and Ben wait. Sam wails.
The tail is off.

Mum pats Sam's cheek. "I can fix this."

Mum tells Sam and Ben she needs
to go.

"Wait!" yells Ben. He runs up to get his ship.

Ben fell. He wails in pain.

The cut is deep. But Mum can fix it.

They get up to go. But Mum needs a wee!

"We can go!" she yells. But the rain is too much.

Mum gets back in. "We will not go
this week."

Ben, Sam and Mum need a nap.

©2021 **BookLife Publishing Ltd.**
King's Lynn, Norfolk PE30 4LS

ISBN 978-1-83927-441-1

Queen Gail Waits & Wait!
Written by Georgie Tennant
Illustrated by Simona Hodonova

An Introduction to BookLife Readers...

Our Readers have been specifically created in line with the London Institute of Education's approach to book banding and are phonetically decodable and ordered to support each phase of Letters and Sounds.

Each book has been created to provide the best possible reading and learning experience. Our aim is to share our love of books with children, providing both emerging readers and prolific page-turners with beautiful books that are guaranteed to provoke interest and learning, regardless of ability.

BOOK BAND GRADED using the Institute of Education's approach to levelling.

PHONETICALLY DECODABLE supporting each phase of Letters and Sounds.

EXERCISES AND QUESTIONS to offer reinforcement and to ascertain comprehension.

BEAUTIFULLY ILLUSTRATED to inspire and provoke engagement, providing a variety of styles for the reader to enjoy whilst reading through the series.

AUTHOR INSIGHT:
GEORGIE TENNANT

Georgie Tennant is a freelance writer who has written multiple stories for BookLife Publishing. She always knew she would be a writer as she used to present her school teachers with lengthy stories and poems for them to enjoy! Her two sons provide plenty of entertaining material for her writing, which usually appears on her blog or in the local newspaper as the 'Thought for the Week'. When she isn't writing she is working as a part-time secondary school English teacher, where she has the joy of inspiring slightly bigger children with the joy of reading good stories. She hopes to write good stories for them one day too.

PHASE 3 /ai/ee/

This book focuses on the phonemes /ai/ and /ee/ and is a yellow level 3 book band.